At a Gallop!

Jen Appleton has managed to win the prize of a lifetime, a two-week cruise to the Caribbean, but will her ship ever set sail with murder and treason afoot?

The dashing Inspector Atkinson enlists her help to track down a killer. But sharing her cabin with a rather bawdy American, Daniel Stapleton, who seems intent on lassoing and *breaking her in,* adds to the mayhem.

Embark on a hap hazardous, slap-stick journey aboard the *Queen Ann.*

Chapter 1: Tips for Selection

Striding triumphantly along the seafront, Jen pulled her suitcase, on its wheels, behind her, admiring the glamorous sight of the Cruise Ship that stood majestically before her. The sea breeze was intense; the saltiness of it filled her nostrils and tickled her taste-buds adding to her jovial holiday mood. Nothing was going to dampen her spirits today, including the horrendous squawking of the seagulls that appeared to be dive-bombing each other overhead.

Although the surroundings were quite industrial, Jen focused only on the magnificent sight of *The Queen Ann* cruise ship, docked in the harbour, alongside some other rather murkier tankers. It was indeed a glorious sight to behold, like an oasis in a desert and she walked sprightly down the jetty into the arrivals lounge, queuing up with other passengers.

The smartly dressed Stewardess greeted her at the counter.

"Good morning Madam. Welcome to *The Queen Ann*. May I have your ticket and your passport please?"

Slightly taken aback at her appearance, Jen grimaced. The amount of makeup that had been shoveled on, as well as that fake smile, but handed her documents over to get them stamped.

"I am so excited to be here. I won the ticket to go on this trip you know, we had a lucky Christmas dip at work. I work for the Jacobson International Media Group in their publishing department. It also stated that if I wanted to bring my partner then it would be fifty percent off for another ticket but who needs one of those?" Jen remarked snorting with laughter, before continuing, "I was a bit worried, that I might get bored on a ship in the middle of the ocean, but then your brochure went on and on about all the activities onboard, to suit my every mood. I have lots of alternative moods. I am a person who likes to be kept constantly active and busy."

"Indeed," the Stewardess replied dryly. "Here is your boarding card, I suggest you hurry along the gangplank then, with everyone else."

Still smiling brightly, at the now bored-looking Stewardess, Jen headed off to join the others. It was a very elegant setting she noted, as she was helped up the gangplank by some stylishly dressed Stewards. There were even more uniformed Stewards a board, directing the passengers where to go, it was all very impressive.

After she had meandered along many cream coloured corridors and up and down some marble steps, adorned with brass banisters, Jen finally arrived at her cabin 38B Deck C and she flung open the door. Disappointed to discover that in her *state-room* she could not swing a cat, she sat on the edge of the bed and unpacked.

Once the task of unpacking had been ticked off her to-do list, she left and got in an elevator to the restaurant level. *The Sea Shell* dining room was smartly dressed in white crisp table clothes and deep red plush carpets with velvety curtains to match. Different types of seashells dotted around the ceiling were indeed a marvel to behold.

Ordering a drink, she wandered to the window and viewed passengers waving to the onlookers onshore. They were about to set sail, she smiled to herself as she looked about the well-appointed restaurant before finishing her drink and getting up.

"Have we left the dock yet?" said a Lady, rather overly ornately dressed as she passed her by. "I haven't felt this dam boat move an inch. It seems like we have been sitting here for hours."

To which Jen replied courteously, "No, but I think everyone is just waving us off now. Oh, that's a rather unhealthy meal your family is eating. I hope all the meals aren't going to be that greasy. Given that I will be on this boat for two weeks, I will probably blow up like a balloon if all the food is going to be as fattening as that."

"Hey the kids love burger and chips," the Lady retorted. "It's our staple diet at home with lots of ketchup."

Raising an eyebrow, Jen surveyed the rather overweight children and a man seated around the table before adding, "Maybe consider cutting down on the salt intake a bit then."

"What a busy body!" shouted the Lady, rather red-faced, glaring angrily up at Jen.

Undeterred, Jen hadn't meant to intentionally upset this family, she actually felt she was trying to be helpful, so she continued on reminding them that people were suffering from coronaries at much younger ages these days. However, this

Lady was having none of it and bellowed across the table.

"Take no notice kids, some people need to mind their business," before she turned to Jen and continued her rant, "Got kids, have you?"

"No, no I haven't," replied Jen rather awkwardly, reflecting that her relationships, as it stood, had not lasted beyond a few months before boredom set in, hence the topic of *having children* had never really come up.

"Well, move on then, really the nerve of some people," sniffed the Lady.

Hurriedly, Jen decided to change the subject, so as to resist the urge to tell her that talking with your mouth full was also considered impolite.

"I won a ticket for this cruise at my workplace," she announced dramatically.

The family, however, ignored her so apologetically she then added, "Of course, I am going, probably best I take a little nap. I had to get up so early to catch this boat."

The family continued to ignore her and the Lady started to sprinkle some more salt over her chips to emphasize her point.

"Right, well I am sure to see you all around, bye."

Taking the hint Jen scurried away.

Using the map on her brochure, Jen made her way back to her room, where she changed into the new pajamas she had purchased especially for this trip, made of a dull, gold satiny material. Playfully diving onto the bed, suddenly she felt incredibly uneasy and reeled back in terror as she had touched down on a solid lumpy mass. Ripping back the sheet and to her absolute horror she discovered, a lifeless face with glassy eyes was staring right back at her.

Bouncing up, alarmed she fell into someone's arms and when she began to scream, hands clutched around her neck. Blindly, she tore the hands from her throat and ran into the corridor. Seeing a big red buzzer, she instinctively pressed it, sirens started going off throughout the boat.

Stewards rushed down the corridors from every direction as Jen frantically pointed into her room. A few minutes later she was taken off by a Stewardess and found herself being seated in the Captain's office.

"Right," said the Captain a thin, lanky chap. "Miss Appleton isn't it? The body in your bed was that your partner?"

"I have never seen that man in my life," replied Jen, still feeling very flustered. "I don't have a boyfriend currently; I am travelling alone."

"Oh, I see," the Captain continued. "Well, we have had to drop anchor now and are barely out of the harbour. The police are on their way to deal with this serious incident. Can I get you a cup of coffee while we wait for them?"

Nodding, Jen accepted his offer but then began pacing around the squeaky clean and sterile whitewashed room. An hour dragged passed before an Inspector Atkinson was finally admitted. He was all manly and rugged as he strode over to Jen in a very decisive and assertive manner.

"Okay Miss Appleton is it?" the Inspector quipped. "No please don't get up, our forensic team is surveying the scene but the ship has been grounded. I am afraid all the passengers are going to have to be interviewed, it is a long and lengthy process. Tests will be run on the body. It may have been simply natural causes but we still need to discover the identity of it as he had no documentation on him. Have a proper think if you know him, Miss Appleton, it will help to speed things up!"

Adamantly, Jen maintained she had never seen that face before. Although the Inspector was dismayed to hear this news, he did then request that the Captain house Miss Appleton elsewhere on the boat.

"Shouldn't we disembark the passengers and put them all up at a hotel in town Inspector?" asked the Captain, who had become very agitated at the bad publicity this whole incident would no doubt conjure up.

"No, the passengers will have to remain on board. No one is allowed to leave until we are satisfied that our inspection of the ship, interrogation of the staff and passengers has reached a satisfactory conclusion," the Inspector replied in a formal tone, folding his arms resolutely.

"That could take hours," the Captain moaned, looking at his watch anxiously.

 This was going to upset his whole time table and his fears only heightened when the Inspector declared it could even take days.

 "We are fully booked however there is a suite that belongs exclusively to an American family, they aren't expected. Miss Appleton could safely stay there overnight." The Captain stated.

 "That's a brilliant idea,' the Inspector concurred, "and I promise to take a proper statement from you later. I am off to check up on the processing of the suite. Maybe some clues have already materialized and we can all clock off early. Rather, unfortunately, they rarely do, so we shall all have to be very brave and sit tight. I am placing this entire ship on lockdown; I fear this is going to be a bumpy ride." The Inspector declared, rather dramatically before sweeping out.

Courteously, Jen was escorted down another long cream drenched corridor, which opened up into a cavernous, vaulted hallway. The Steward then unlocked a double set of oak wooden doors, with a gold leaf sign upon them which stated simply that this was the 'Stapleton Suite'. Reassuring her that she was going to be extremely comfortable in there. The Stapleton's, she was informed, were wealthy and although they had been renting out this suite for years, had in fact barely ever used it. But Jen wasn't interested in the use of their facilities, she just wanted a lie-down, it had all still been such a dreadful shock.

However, when the door opened, Jen's jaw dropped, sprawling out before her was such a decadent setting, very different to her suite. The scene that had unravelled before her was so dazzling that Jen didn't know where to look first. There was a luxurious spacious lounge with a horsey theme going on, judging by the number of pictures and statues about. This equine stuff seemed rather odd though since they were on a cruise ship after all.

Next, to catch her attention was a raised state of the art kitchen and a lot of double doors leading to who knows where? The Steward led her to a double bedroom, off the lounge, before taking his leave of her.

Chapter 2: Consider Your Position

The opulent bedroom décor impressed Jen, allowing herself a roll on to the bed. Reveling in her millionaire moment, enjoying the feel of the silk sheets around her, she temporarily forgot about the horrific start to her day and she slowly drifted off. Suddenly she was awakened by the force of a body jumping upon her, she sat up alarmed and screamed, thinking it was a murderer coming to kill her.

"Hey calm down lady. Who the hell are you?" asked a mid-twenties American accented male, with golden brown, curly short locks and blue sparkling eyes.

"I should be asking you that question, who are you?" she remarked before noticing other young ladies that surrounded him, on the bed, of similar age to him.

"I am Malcolm Stapleton and this is my room."

   Embarrassed, Jen was immediately apologetic. Quickly she introduced herself explaining, "A man's lifeless body has been found in my cabin, which has left me as a witness to a possible murder. The Captain said I could use this suite, apparently, it is never occupied."

"Yes, that is true we rarely use it. I just show up out of the blue occasionally, as I don't need a booking, we own this suite. I wanted to show it off to my little beauties here but a murder, how exciting. Well, we are here to play, have some fun and games. You can join in with us while you're waiting if you want?" Malcolm mentioned brightly.

Slowly Jen surveyed the three ladies, clad in very short loose-fitting outfits around her. Her mind assessed what sort of fun and games they could have in mind, concluding it would most definitely not amuse her.

"My name is Strawberry," announced one young lady.

"I am Cherry," stated another.

"Oh God, please don't tell me your banana," Jen stated somewhat sarcastically pulling her sheet away from her.

"No Apricot," the final female giggled.

Feeling frazzled, Jen declined the offer, to participate in their *fun and games session*, instead climbed over Strawberry in order to scurry out of the room. Resentful of their intrusion, she strode over to the kitchen and started to make a cup of coffee.

Speedily Malcolm opened the double doors and closing them behind him wandered up the stairs toward her. Once again, she apologized for the interruption.

"It's all fine," Malcolm reassured her, "I was getting a bit bored of the girls anyway. I have left them to play with each other. This is so intriguing, a murder. You will have to give me all the juicy details. Perhaps together we can solve this mystery. I have always wanted to play the role of detective. So first tell me a bit about yourself, I will need to rule you out."

"I never met the victim and there is not a lot to say about me Malcolm, other than I work for a Media company. I have a junior management position in their publishing department. The rest is now all a bit of a blur. I am still in shock from discovering a dead body in my cabin. Inspector Atkinson will be along here shortly, to take my statement, then I will be out of your hair."

"Oh, don't be like that, I want you to stay. An Inspector eh, I hope he is one of those tall, muscular and handsome detectives. Like that *Inspector Lewis* I have seen on British TV,"

Malcolm cooed sitting with his head in his hands watching her sip her drink.

"Well I was too overwhelmed at the time to view him in that light, but now you come to mention it, he was quite dashing," Jen replied. "Quite clean-cut and tall with blond swept up hair."

"Wow he sounds truly exciting," Malcolm gushed.

Suddenly there was a knock at the door, Inspector Atkinson marched in with a female constable at his side and approached them. Apologizing for keeping her waiting, Jen introduced him to Malcolm. Gallantly, the Inspector thanked Malcolm for being obliging enough to allow Miss Appleton to stay in his suite, but Malcolm reassured him that it was his pleasure, declaring he found detective work fascinating.

The Inspector asked Malcolm to call him Ron which caused Malcolm to blush. They shook hands and momentarily eyed each other up.

"Do you mind me staying Inspector, I have never seen an interview of a witness to a murder before." Malcolm requested, "Jen I am sure will find it a support." The Inspector readily agreed, so they seated themselves around a large, dark mahogany dining room table, in the center of the lounge.

"Okay Miss Appleton, can you give me a detailed account of what happened. Constable Mately here will write down your statement, given that you are still in shock, then you will read it. Hopefully, if you are happy with it sign it," stated the Inspector assertively.

"Please call me Jen. As I recall, I went up to the restaurant at 7:30 a.m. and got a juice before returning to my room and changing for bed. I didn't fully strip off as this was just meant to be a short nap so I still had my underwear on, thank goodness with all the people that have been around me so far today."

 She laughed nervously.

"Do you normally change for bed in the morning Jen?" remarked the Inspector, slightly taken back. Malcolm, however, had a gleam of amusement in his eye at her comment.

"No," Jen replied. "It was just well, coming all the way down to the Southampton Docks from London meant I had to catch numerous trains and wake up exceptionally early. I was hoping for a long nap so I wanted to dress comfortably, before getting up and joining in with all the rejuvenating activities that this ship has to offer. I like to be kept busy. I jumped up on my bed and suddenly found myself straddling this dead body."

Swiftly Malcolm put his arm around her shoulders, to offer comfort.

"Sorry Jen, look I better phone my dad and let him know what is going on. I promise to catch up with you later. I hope to see you around too Inspector."

"I will need to get a statement from you later Malcolm," the Inspector noted. "Go on Jen."

"Then, I pulled back the sheet and saw these glassy eyes staring up at me, I screamed and fell back or did I get off the bed not sure, but these hands were suddenly around my neck." Jen anxiously commented and she began to fidget in her chair at the terrifying recollection.

"So, there was another person in the room?" the Inspector gasped sharply, rising up to deliberate on this new piece of information.

"Yes, I think so," Jen responded, with some hesitation in her voice. "Unless my mind had gone into some sort of hysterical overload, I have never seen a dead body. I ran out of the room and pushed on what I presumed to be an emergency button."

"Yes, that was a security button. But what about the person? Which way did they run off to?" the Inspector asked impatiently, placing his hands on the rim of the leather-backed chair as he studied her.

"I never actually saw anyone and then all these Stewards were about assisting me."

Noting that she was still looking quite pale, the Inspector suggested she go off to get some sleep.

Irritated, Jen remarked, "I have been trying to do that Inspector, but then Malcolm and his *fruit salad* landed up on top of me in the bed. I am concerned about where I am going to be sent to now, in order to get some rest. Given that Malcolm is obviously going to occupy the bedroom."

"In a suite this size Miss Appleton, there is bound to be another bedroom, so I advise you not to stress about it too much. We are still waiting to hear if this dead man, was killed under suspicious circumstances. They are running his fingerprints through the system to gain his identity, but as all of this will take time, you will definitely be staying here overnight."

Then, Jen continued with her statement and after reading it, signed it as Malcolm came bounding back into the room.

"My father is flying in; he will be landing his helicopter on deck shortly. He always likes to make a spectacular entrance. So, is it my turn now Inspector?" he announced cheerfully, planting himself on a chair next to Jen.

"Just a formality really Malcolm. How long have you been on the ship?" the Inspector inquired walking over and sitting opposite him.

Responding somewhat cagily Malcolm replied, "I arrived this morning about 8:30 a.m. with girlfriends, I think or maybe it was earlier or even later. My mind has gone blank. My friends are currently playing in my bedroom. We did some bowling, had breakfast upstairs in the Mexican themed restaurant, before crashing in here and interrupting Jen's sleep. Sorry about that Jen."

"Do you normally carry on in such a reckless manner?" the Inspector questioned quite sharply.

"Excuse me, Inspector, that is a bit of a personal question. I have just been having a laugh with some friends, that is not against the law is it?"

The men's eyes met and narrowed they were definitely weighing each other up, trying to get the measure of one another. Jen looked back and forth between them, it was like a tennis match, the atmosphere was electric between the two.

"I am merely pointing out Malcolm, that someone of your stature could be spending his time a bit more productively."

The Inspector glanced through the spiral-bound book, that the constable had been making her notes in, before returning his expressionless gaze to Malcolm.

"Oh my God, you sound like my father," Malcolm wailed, "and he's not been a great role model. First, he married my mother then he took up with a load of Philippine women. So, although I have had a privileged upbringing Inspector, there has also been a complete lack of stability in my childhood. Thanks a lot for bringing all that out of me. I am feeling quite depressed now."

Getting up the Inspector walked around the table. Patting Malcolm on the shoulder to comfort him, he then requested that he call out his friends so that he could question them, which Malcolm duly did.

They all sat around the table except for Jen who had shifted to the kitchen. She was pacing up and down deep in thought when the noise of a helicopter landing could be heard and it shattered the conversation at the table. A few minutes later an extremely broad-shouldered, medium built man, with a Stetson on his head, entered the suite.

"Oh, hi dad," Malcolm shouted racing over to embrace his father. "Please take off the Stetson, you are giving us Americans an awful image. We aren't all cowboys toting guns."

"Oh, come on son *John Wayne* did that already and you know your dad likes to fly the flag. It is freezing cold here in Britain. I don't care if it's their summer," replied his father, rather loudly. "I see the suite is packed; hi I am Daniel but please Malcolm introduce me to everyone."

"This is Inspector Ron Atkinson, Ron this is my dad Daniel and then these three are my playmates Apricot, Cherry and Strawberry. Oh, that is

Constable Mately, she is here to take statements," Malcolm responded in a giddy over-excited manner.

"How about that one?" asked Daniel nodding his head toward Jen. "Pacing up and down like a Mustang caught in a pen. Hey, let us see if she responds to this?"

  With that, Daniel made this low clicking sound and Jen threw her head back, stopped and turned towards the group watching her, a piece of her long black fringe fell across her eye.

"Well I will be damned she does," he laughed incredulously.

"That is Jen dad, the little Brit I was telling you about, who has to stay here as her room has a dead body in it," Malcolm commented matter-of-factly, smiling warmly toward her.

"Okay little Brit, come over here and say hello then. Oh, my God did you just snort at me, young lady?" Daniel inquired as Jen came over to him, extending out her hand.

"Sorry, but I am a little surprised at your bad manners that is all. Why can't you walk over to greet me? Not very gentlemanly. Obviously, a man used to getting his own way."

  Amused Daniel took up her hand to shake it. Taking a moment to critically appraise her, reckoning she was around her mid-thirties and in good shape. This unnerved her, causing a furrow too appear between her brow, so she took a few steps back when he finally released her hand.

"That is my dad Jen, get used to it." Malcolm joked. "He spends all his time at his ranch with his precious horses so is not accustomed to mixing with polite society."

  Still laughing, Malcolm returned to sit with his friends and the Inspector at the table, leaving Daniel and Jen still facing each other. How to describe Daniel, Jen mused, over-confident, over-bearing and over-here. Turning Daniel called over to his son.

"My stay at the ranch was cut short this time by you Malcolm, just hopping on a plane and disappearing off. I have had to chase you all over the Atlantic. Won't you ever settle down boy?"

"Not now dad, I am sure not everybody in this room wants to hear about how overprotective you are of me."

  Nervously Malcolm glanced around him.

 "We are going out for a drink at the bar if you have no objections dad. Do you want to come, Ron? Oh yeah, I forgot you are on duty."

"I am actually about to knock off so I wouldn't mind joining you. How about you Jen?" asked the Inspector as he trailed his eyes over to her.

"I am hardly dressed for it am I? Look at me. I have spent most of the day in my pajamas. Any chance I could nip back to my room quickly and grab my clothes? I won't take a minute I promise," Jen begged.

  "I am afraid that will not be possible. All your belongings have been sealed away. I can send the constable here out to town to get you some outfits. It shouldn't be that difficult a task given that the Ship has yet to leave the harbour."

Interrupting the Inspector, Daniel put in, that he had some outfits in his bedroom that would do.

Given that this loud, bawdy man had not made a good first impression on Jen, she responded quite tersely, to his generous offer by stating,

"I don't think I will fit into outfits from the Philippines, they are very petite out there aren't they? What was their average age than eighteen?"

This statement caused Daniel to glare angrily over at his son, who in turn winced and cast his eyes down.

"Wow, little Brit was that your first warning shot?" Daniel retorted, stung slightly by her sarcastic remark but recovering quickly. "No, I think they will fit your frame. My room is over there. Okay well see you guys later, I will wait for the little Brit and meet you up there."

Quietly Malcolm then spoke to his father aside, "Just to warn you, dad, I saw that acquaintance of yours, Jane Camberley on the Ship, I think she saw me too but I ducked down trying to avoid her. Those hugs she keeps giving me, even as a kid they were always a bit too intense."

Daniel listened as he watched Jen take the steps two at a time and she entered his room as the others left. An intense feeling of sheer exhilaration swelled up in his chest, it had been a while since he had felt that aroused.

Chapter 3: Thoroughbred or not?

Quite sprightly Jen came down the stairs, a few minutes later in a cream linen knee-length dress. Upon her arrival, back in the lounge, she informed him that although this dress did fit all the shoes were too tiny for her feet.

"Well as you now find yourself in a predicament with no shoes to wear, let us stay in. You can cook for me if you like." Daniel suggested.

Although Jen did feel the need to eat, she was annoyed to find herself left alone with him. But then his voice softened and Jen felt more at ease as he encouraged her, in low tones to slow down, so she responded hesitantly, agreeing to his plan.

Smiling he watched her skittishly jumping about him busily making them some sandwiches.

"Not quite sure if cheese and tomato sandwiches are your thing, but given my day I am not quite up to making anything else." She replied handing him a plate of them. He then noticed her take some purposeful slow steps toward him and he impulsively extended his hand out to pat her forearm, she flinched and threw back her head.

"Hey you are a bit skittish," Daniel remarked, placing his plate on the counter and strolling forward to close the distance between them.

"I had a wild Mustang like you once and when it came to breaking her in, I had to ride her real hard." His voice sounded quite husky

Unfazed by the obvious innuendo Jen replied.

"Drop down dead after that, did she?"

"No," Daniel mused retrieving his plate, "it took a few rides but I eventually broke her in."

"I certainly hope you are not equating me with a horse. Mr. Yank," she retaliated before munching down on her sandwich.

"Hey, it's Daniel."

As they settled to eat their meal Daniel poured them both a glass of red wine.

"That dress you chose to wear actually belonged to my previous wife Charlene. She's dead."

This revelation caused Jen to start choking slightly, on her sandwich and she took a swig of her wine to settle herself.

"Malcolm's mother died in a boating accident nearly fifteen years ago now. I was on the boat with her when we were caught in a storm and it capsized. Not a great time for Malcolm, growing up without a mother," Daniel remarked, scooping up the last morsel on his plate.

"I am sorry for your loss," Jen commented as Daniel continued, an amused smile flicked across his lips.

"Yeah so, I simply drifted about after that, in and out of relationships. As Malcolm stated I had a few long-term commitments with Philippine women. What the hell, they were very obliging."

"And no doubt subservient," Jen commented sharply, standing up to remove both their empty dishes and take them over to the sink.

"Hell yeah, so tell me about your romantic escapades then little Brit," chuckled Daniel.

Then Jen rounded on him.

"Okay, well I actually had grown-up relationships with people of my own age!"

"Wow!" Daniel laughed. "Is that yet another warning shot. I duly note your sarcastic tone. You really know how to let off a round."

Rearing her head back to look at him her long fringe fells across her face again, he half-smiled and looked away as Jen replied,

"You will excuse my bad manners but I didn't come here tonight to divulge the ins and outs of my love life to you, a complete stranger."

With that, she sauntered down to the lounge and began to pace about.

"Oh, I don't know about that complete stranger bit little Brit I think I am slowly getting the measure of you. Definitely a Mustang in a previous life," he mentioned smirking at her.

Daniel found it fascinating observing her prancing around him, hurling sarcastic comments his way.

Swiftly, Jen responded to this statement by declaring that she had *grazed enough now* and she enquired as to where she would be sleeping.

Generously Daniel offered her his room, stating that they were both adults after all. She was not quite sure what to make of that remark so she chose to ignore it, commenting only that she would be *trotting off to bed now.*

Gazing intently Daniel watched her as she took another set of steps two at a time up to his room and a wolfish grin appeared on his face. The following morning Jen rolled over in her bed and saw Daniel sitting up reading from a Kindle right next to her. Turning he smiled down sardonically at her.

"Shit Daniel!" she exclaimed gripping the sheet and pulling it around her. "I thought you were going to take another room or at least sleep on the couch."

"I did say we were both adults, eh little Brit," he sniggered. "Good morning to you too. Did I harm you overnight?"

"No but…." Jen responded begrudgingly. She looked over to him but the tension between them began to build.

"Well don't be so skittish about this then," he interrupted her and his jaw tightened. "You are meant to be learning to trust me, it's your first training session little Brit. Did you just snort at me again?"

Haughtily Jen crossed the wooden parquet flooring into the bathroom. Before taking a shower, she made sure the door was bolted behind her. A little while later she re-emerged in his room in a towel dressing gown.

"You should choose something else to wear. There is fresh underwear in there too," Daniel advised pointing across the room.

"I am feeling a bit ghoulish about the whole matter," Jen complained.

However, Daniel reassured her that all the clothes were clean and there was no one else around to make use of them. Reluctantly, Jen went into the walk-in wardrobe to select an outfit but returned back still in the towel dressing gown.

"Nothing in there seems to suit, the majority of it is floral print dresses no doubt mementos from your Philopena era. It's not the type of clothes that I would normally wear. I will just put that linen dress on again. Actually, I do prefer trousers, I feel safe and secure in trousers."

"Oh, you mean long pants, sure it might take me longer to wrestle those off you but I am up for the challenge," Daniel replied suggestively.

Although Jen did not find this particular joke funny, so frowned at him, she did retrieve some fresh underwear from a draw and picking up the dress, went to change in the bathroom. Upon her return to the room however, she found Daniel completely naked with his back to her, picking out clothes very matter-of-factly. Not knowing where to look, she proceeded swiftly to the door.

"Do you think I should wear blue today, the colour of my eyes?" he asked completely unabashed, holding up a shirt on a hanger. Jen turned and saw his bare, firm torso.

"I think you should act your age, Daniel."

Hurriedly she stormed out, slamming the door deliberately behind her. Relieved to see Malcolm, Jen wandered over wishing him a good morning.

"Hi Jen, we had a great night, you should have come. That Inspector, I mean Ron was such good fun last night. Did you just come out of my dad's bedroom?" asked Malcolm, suddenly aghast.

"Yes, but obviously nothing happened, we only shared a bed to sleep on," she replied flatly.

"Wow, I didn't realize my dad was such a fast mover. There is life in the old dog yet, as they say," Malcolm chortled.

Ignoring his comment, Jen made herself a coffee.

Suddenly Daniel called across the room, "Hey little Brit make me one of those, I take it black."

Springing up the steps to the kitchen he sat beside his son as Jen handed him a coffee.

"Okay gentlemen, I have a really busy day ahead of me. I am off to assist Inspector Atkinson with his investigations. I always like to lend a hand. I am confident that with my help the process will speed up and I will be sleeping in my own bed tonight. So, see you both much later on then, bye."

"It's been so lovely to meet you, Jen. Stay in touch." Malcolm cooed. Daniel was staring intently at her, however, she refused to make any sort of eye contact with him as she found his behaviour very unnerving. Hurriedly striding across the room, she left the suite without another utterance.

Still, in a cheerful mood, Malcolm commented on how lovely he had so far found the British people to be. However, his dad mentioned his concern about the friends that were currently flaunting themselves around his son's bedroom. Malcolm became quite indignant about this.

"Since when have my lifestyle habits bothered you?" Malcolm complained. "As it happens, they had a row and I ended up sleeping out here watching the TV. All that shouting at each other gave me a headache. How about you, sleeping with a woman you have only just met. What a great role model you are dad."

With that Malcolm moved away from his father, in annoyance and plonked himself down on the couch with his back toward him.

"Little Brit, she's great eh,"

Daniel smirked his pleasure still clearly evident.

"I don't think she is that into you though dad," Malcolm muttered as he lay back and rested his head on the cushions.

"She's only being a bit skittish. I will take it slowly and gently until she comes around, get her all relaxed first," Daniel replied as a mischievous expression appeared on his face.

"Dad she isn't one of your horses, she is a human being."

Groaning Malcolm picked up the TV remote and began flicking through the channels. *The Inspector Lewis show* came on and he settled down to watch that as his father came over and sat by him.

"It's a compliment Malcolm, you know how much I value my horses. Now, what plans do you have for us today."

"How about a jog around the ship and a session in the spa's hot tub?" Malcolm suggested and his dad *heartily* agreed.

The ballroom had been set up as an incident room and as people came and went Jen sat with Inspector Atkinson. Helpfully Jen assisted Constable Mately by taking notes when she went on breaks. Quite intrigued by the ongoings of the investigation, Jen also sat at other tables listening to other people's recounted tales of what they were up to on the fateful day. It felt like a long morning and finally when Inspector Atkinson was done, he walked her back to the Stapleton suite, whereupon she invited him in for coffee as the other men returned.

"Where's your fruit salad gone Malcolm?" Jen joked.

His bedroom doors were flung open revealing the empty space.

"My friends have gone for a relaxing massage and pampering session at the Sanctuary Spa. I expect they will be here shortly."

Feeling this was a great idea Jen disappeared off to Malcolm's room, off the lounge, to borrow something to wear from the *fruit salads'* collection.

"Bloody Hell, that Jen was hard work today," the Inspector confessed. "Do you mind keeping her at home with you guys tomorrow? Talk about hindering an investigation, she was up and down the tables all day interrogating people."

Daniel and Malcolm laughed as Ron continued, "Within two hours she had a list of suspects as long as your arm. One man left in tears, she felt she recognized his scent from the scene but his arms were too short to reach up to her neck."

This caused Daniel and Malcolm's laughter to increase.

"She really was a riot, kept us all amused."

Happily, Daniel concurred with the Inspector's assessment by remarking that she was indeed a handful, really highly strung and temperamental, he wondered why someone hadn't broken her in a long while back.

The Inspector then stated, "I wouldn't wish that on any bloke mate."

They all found that comment hilariously funny until Jen abruptly stepped forward in front of them, from Malcolm's open bedroom.

"Well thanks a lot, guys, I heard all of that. Making a public nuisance of myself, was I? When I was only trying to be of assistance! That was really stupid of me eh!" she cried out and turned to gain some composure.

The Inspector attempted to get up but Daniel put his arm across him barring his way and said,

"Don't rush her or she will bolt. Come over here little Brit, settle and we can talk about this. We are all very sorry that you heard that."

Pacing up and down, Jen then gazed down at her feet, by the front door momentarily lost for words, she turned up to look at them very flushed.

"Really is that what you think about me? All having a good laugh, how humiliating. How am I meant to ever show my face around here again! You all just think I am so ridiculous, a joke."

Attempting to take control of the situation, Daniel spoke in low soft tones, "Just calm yourself down, let's discuss this quietly. Come on little Brit settle down."

So, Jen took a few tentative steps towards them but then Malcolm jumped out of his seat and came careering toward her.

"Jen oh Jen we are sorry," Malcolm cried out in a pleading tone with his arms outstretched, ready to embrace her.

Throwing back her head Jen replied "No Malcolm don't just don't," before she turned and stormed out the front door, nearly bumping into Cherry, Apricot and Strawberry at the doorway.

They walked right into Malcolm and started hugging him.

Chapter 4: Are They The Right Temperament?

The inspector got up, declaring that he would go and deal with this but Daniel was already one step ahead of him and called out,

"It's okay Inspector, I have got this. You will only spook her; I understand her temperament."

But Malcolm shouted after his father, "Dad she is not a bloody horse."

However, Daniel continued racing after Jen down the corridor, easily overtaking her and put his arms out either side of himself, to slow her down.

"It's okay little Brit, take it easy, slow down and talk to me."

Again, he spoke in low soft tones.

"Bloody men all think I am so funny," Jen said exasperatedly.

Still walking backward with his arms outstretched, Daniel slowed his pace, she too was then forced to slow down. Eventually, she did come to a complete halt, but then began walking in circles in small steps looking at her feet.

"Am I such a joke to all of you then?" she eventually muttered.

"No of course not," Daniel reassured her. "We were only letting off a bit of steam, come here let me rub those tense shoulders." Placing his hands on her shoulders, he massaged into them. He spoke quietly in her ear,

"It's okay little Brit, it is all going to be okay."

His soft-spoken words and murmurings did help soothe her and then he turned her gently so that she was facing his chest and he placed his arms about her. Softly he stroked her long black hair, still whispering reassurances in her ear, but then a woman cried out breaking the spell between them.

"Oh my God Daniel is that you?" a female American voice shrieked out. "Wow Daniel that is you, come here and give me a hug."

"Hi Jane," Daniel said to a short, muscular, blonde woman approaching him. "Wow, it's great to see you too. I am in the middle of something right now, however."

Suddenly, he felt Jen's muscles tense up, she raised her head to pull away from him.

"Hey I know we didn't leave on great terms buddy, but you are still looking as handsome as ever you old rogue," Jane chuckled before turning her attentions to Jen to remark cuttingly, "Daniel and I have known each other for years, always in and out of each other's private lives, eh Daniel."

"This isn't great timing right now Jane, my friend here is a bit upset," Daniel stated firmly.

"No, it's a perfect time Daniel," Jen said nervously. "Please, you spend some time with your friend catching up. I always like to be alone at humiliating times like this, it helps me to process, lick my wounds and get back in the saddle, so to speak."

With that, she started walking backward away from them before turning to hurriedly speed away.

"Okay great Daniel, it looks like I am all yours for the evening then," Jane declared gleefully moving swiftly forward and reaching for his hand.

"No Jane no, my friend really does need a friend right now, even if she doesn't realize it, so I will catch up with you later. Tomorrow, maybe we can play some tennis. I will see you."

Leaving Jane feeling somewhat disconcerted, by his impulsive behavior, Daniel resumed his chase. Eventually catching up with her.

"Come on little Brit just settle, come on slow down."

"I said I was fine Daniel; you can go back and play with your playmate of the month I just ..."

However, Daniel interrupted her by saying quietly, "Just what little Brit? Want to beat up on yourself some more, come here. That massage was helping to soothe you, walk with me."

Taking her by the hand and noticing a first aid sign on a door, he pulled her into a small medical room, with a high bed in it for patients to lie on.

Noticing her startled expression, he quickly declared, "No, I don't want you to lie on the bed, but lay against it, so I can rub away those tense back muscles," he said stalking closer and he shuffled her around to face the bed.

As Jen bent forward slightly to lay on part of the bed, he began to massage her back. He moved right up into her as she felt his fingers work their magic on the tight knots within her tense muscles. Then he heard her let out a sigh and smiled as he felt her relaxing. Mischievously, he continued to speak in soft low reassuring tones to her.

"You like that don't you girl, just settle and relax this is going to make you feel a whole lot better."

Suddenly Jen heard a clicking and rasping sound, she stirred uncomfortably but his strong hands spread over her again and his soft words were still telling her to settle. She was feeling in a calm memorized state, when she felt the skin of his hand brush down against the cheek of her buttock and his fingers entered into her pants, she snapped up and around angrily to face him.

"What the bloody hell are you doing Daniel?" she yelled at him.

  At that moment, her hands were on his chest pushing him firmly back, it was as if she had reared up at him and as he stumbled his jeans fell around his ankles.

'Oh my God, here I am in a distressed state and all you are doing is thinking about fucking me, really Daniel you are unbelievable."

  Hitching up his jeans, he backed away as she *flipped out*, kicking away the chair that was now between them.

"Maybe we should call Jane back in and have a threesome is that what you would like Daniel? No don't even answer that or try to talk to me and attempt to defend yourself. Leave me alone."

Watching her bolt out of the room, Daniel admitted defeat. Buckling up his belt, he put his hat back on and returned to the corridor, where he noticed Jane was still hovering about.

"Hey, Jane do you fancy coming to get a drink with me? I feel like getting totally wasted tonight."

Agreeing, Jane willing went off with him to find the nearest watering hole. In the meantime, Jen had caught a glimpse of Malcolm through a window of a bar. She entered the overly reddishly decorated surroundings with rather garish chandeliers overhead and followed a pathway flanked by railings. Carefully she moved toward Malcolm's table situated at the far end in a corner, noticing, in disbelief, he was actually holding hands with Ron they appeared to be necking. They leaped apart as Jen approached them. The song *You have placed a chill in my hear*" by the Eurythmics was playing in the background.

Quickly Malcolm jumped up to reiterate that they were both really sorry about what had happened that day.

"This is turning out to be a real crap day," Jen remarked despondently. "Were you two just kissing each other? Maybe it's me, I am feeling so dizzy or am I just hallucinating?"

 Cautiously Ron replied, "No Jen we were, so you can now go and get your own back on me, by reporting it."

"What would be the point of doing that?" Jen responded. "Shove over and buy me a drink I want to drown my sorrows."

"Oh Christ," Malcolm said. "There is my dad and I am still not ready to tell him about me being gay yet. Let's get out of here."

  Readily Jen agreed to leave, Daniel was certainly the last person she wanted to be near right now too. So, Ron suggested they go back to their suite for drinks and he led them off. In the meantime, Daniel was offering Jane a stool at the bar and helping her up onto it. Giggling as he lifted her up, Jane then turned to the bartender to order herself a drink.

 Scanning the bar Daniel saw the Inspector, Jen, and Malcolm approaching. They tried steering themselves passed him, but he jumped off from his stool to block their path.

"What's this I see Jen, are you making up your own little threesome tonight?" Daniel commented acidly.

  This caused Malcolm to completely turn on his dad, "I can't believe those words came out of your mouth. You had better keep it shut as Jen has been through enough tonight, without you adding to it, don't you think dad?".

 Slowly Daniel withdrew and returned to have a drink with Jane. However, her constant chatter soon went over his ears, so he found himself paying for the drinks and wishing her goodnight. When she bent forward to give him a farewell kiss, she was dismayed to find that he had already gone. The bartender ended up having to walk around the counter, to assist her off the stool.

   Eventually returning to his suite, Daniel found that the Inspector at the door already leaving. Pausing, Ron gave Daniel a slight nod before he wandered off.   When Daniel entered, he noticed Jen helping herself to a large glass of red wine and Malcolm was opening a bottle of Smirnoff red.

"Okay Malcolm, I am here to make my peace, can you give me and little Brit some space?" he asked standing in the center of the lounge with his hands on his hips.

"I can't believe you spoke to her like that dad. I am so shocked. You shouted that out in front of everybody at the bar. Believe me, I have already apologized to Jen a number of times. I am so ashamed of you."

   So, Daniel reassured his son that he did not come back to cause any further trouble. Quietly Malcolm asked Jen if she would be okay for his dad to have a word with her, without him present and she nodded.

"I can take care of myself Malcolm, goodnight, I will see you in the morning."

The atmosphere was quite tense, so Malcolm, seeing them both glaring at each other decided to make a hurried exit to his room.

Quickly, Jen downed her second glass of wine and felt a bit merrier so she raised her head to look across at Daniel defiantly. She walked confidently down the steps, strolled slowly into the lounge to face him.

"So, you said you want to say something to me, well I am standing right here so say it," she taunted him.

Slowly Daniel moved around her, his arms folded, taking his time to speak. As he circled around her, she fidgeted restlessly before him, doing some short sideways step away from him as he began to address her.

"I am not going to lie to you little Brit. I did want to take you tonight, I am really drawn to you and I should regret it, I know."

"Okay Daniel, so this strong attraction you have can be extinguished if we actually then just go for it and have sex," Jen teased.

Finally, she made eye contact with him.

"Wow I was not expecting that!" he remarked but maintained his fixed gaze at her.

"No come-on Daniel," she declared in a more challenging tone. "Time to put your money where your mouth is. We have sex this whole fantasy of yours then diminishes."

"Are you offering to have ssssex with me?" stammered Daniel becoming rather aroused.

"Yes, why not? We do it, it's then case closed. Everyone can move on with their business."

Swinging her head around to face him, her fringe fell across half her face as he approached her.

"Well I am up for it, let's go, the sooner I get you out of my system the better," he said firmly.

This caused Jen to back up slightly, as the sight of his massive frame, right before her promptly made her completely revise her proposal.

"I think there may be one slight problem," she piped up. "My feet feel suddenly stuck in the mud. Shame could have been such an interesting night."

Not to be outdone by, however, Daniel who by now was consumed by arousal, bent over to scoop her up in his arms before he carried her up the stairs. Kicking open his bedroom doors and depositing her on the bed. He turned to close the doors behind him. Stunned by his actions, she watched him undress with wide eyes and then he moved to retrieve a condom from his bedside table drawer.

Her head went down and her nostrils flared. "You put those fingers down there and I will bite them off."

Sneering Daniel looked up at her, "Yeah I bet you would bite me too, my little Mustang."

"That round goes to you then but be warned, now I am on to your game; I will break you in."

With that, he rolled over smirking and slept.

Trusting he would now behave Jen slept beside him. However, during the course of the night, she was awoken by the sound of moans. It appeared Daniel was having some sort of nightmare and she moved over to him. By this point, Jen didn't feel so threatened by him anymore and relaxed into him. Carefully she spoke softly into his ear reassuring words and her hand caressed his chest. When she felt him settle, she started to move her hand away but he suddenly grasped hold of it. Turning he looked up at her quite sharply causing her to withdraw.

"You were having some sort of nightmare, I wanted to comfort you," Jen murmured.

Leaning over her he began kissing her deeply on the mouth. Then he pulled his body once again over hers and began pressing down upon it.

A sigh of satisfaction escaped her lips, he noted strengthening his resolve.

But she gently untangled herself from him, pushing him away and half laughed at him, nervously putting on the towel dressing gown, she left the room.   Wandering through to the lounge, out the French windows to sit on the balcony.

Dawn was breaking over the cargo ships and although there was a rather unpleasant odour being emitted from them, she sighed, realizing that her life would never be quite the same again.

Chapter 5: Get To Know Their Personality

Sometime later Malcolm appeared at the doorway.

"Morning Jen, I am making coffees do you want one?"

"I would love one, thanks, Malcolm."

"The noise of those seagulls is enough to bring on a migraine. Hey did my dad behave himself with you last night, after I left?" he innocently asked.

"No worries Malcolm, I managed to rope and brand him," she replied.

Smiling Malcolm returned to the kitchen; his father approached him.

"Do you want a coffee dad?"

"No, it's okay son, I will get my little Brit to make me one later she likes keeping busy. Where has she bolted off to this morning do you know?"

Daniel surveyed the vacant area.

"She's outpacing around the back there. But dad I really think you need to slow down. Jen is a bit, I think the expression is straight-laced."

Giving a short laugh before responding, "She's my Mustang you can take my word for it."

Jen was indeed pacing around outside, wondering how on earth she was going to face Daniel this morning and then suddenly there he was in the doorway, her head reared up and her long fringe settled in its usual position across her face. Giving a wry smile before approaching her, caused Jen to back right up to the steel railings, on the balcony.

"Was that a good morning snort I just heard?" Daniel asked Jen who then twirled around turning her back to him.

Gripping on to the railings, Jen contemplated leaping off but judging the drop decided against it. Then Daniel was suddenly right up against her, his hands on either side of the rail as his body encased hers.

"That second round I definitely bagged you last night," he whispered into her ear, delighting in the nervous energy that exuded from her body.

"As if!" Jen huffed, "We can call it a tie then game over."

"The race has not even begun yet my little Mustang. So, what are our plans for today?" he smugly replied.

Rolling her eyes, the thought of having to spend the day with him, it sent a quiver down her spine.

Momentarily, she glanced down at the ornate tiled flooring before returning her steely gaze at him.

"Well Daniel, I had planned to go shopping today and buy myself a chastity belt."

This sharp statement caused Dan to howl with laughter at her, but Jen found herself feeling even more suffocated by him, as she tried desperately to wriggle free.

"Seriously Jen that kiss last night was totally unexpected, really pleasurable."

"Well bravo," Jen stated. "I am so glad you thoroughly enjoyed yourself, not that there is going to be an encore, now if you would excuse me my coffee is getting cold."

"Hey I like mine black don't forget," he casually requested.

When she felt his body relax back, she bolted out from under his armpit and arrived in the kitchen quite breathless. After she accepted the coffee, given to her by Malcolm, she settled herself at the table opposite him. There was a knock at the door and Inspector Atkinson strode in. They greeted him as he joined them at the table.

"How is the investigation going Inspector? I am hoping that something has developed in the case, so we can all resume our normal lives, I am beginning to get cabin fever," Jen commented, the agitation in her voice clear to all.

"Well we now know the name of the dead man which is a start, Lord Bellington," the Inspector commented, taking off his coat and placing it around the brightly steel-framed kitchen chair.

"Oh, even I have heard of him," Malcolm said. "He had quite a large presence in the gay scene."

"I hardly think so, he was in the papers last year as there was a huge scandal involving him and the wife of a prominent MP," the Inspector declared as Jen got up to make more coffee.

"Do you always believe what you read in the tabloids, Ron? I promise you he was as gay as us," Malcolm replied.

Politely, Jen handed the Inspector a coffee.

"Well that has thrown a spanner in the works then Malcolm, I am going to have to take you in for questioning," the Inspector remarked, helping himself to milk and sugar on the table.

"I am not a suspect, am I?" Malcolm shrieked, crossing his legs and fidgeting about nervously in his seat.

"I am sure you have a perfectly innocent explanation for this Malcolm," stated Jen comfortingly.

"I do," Malcolm informed them, "I have never actually met Lord Bellington."

The Inspector assured him that it was, *purely routine* for Malcolm to come in and assist with the investigation.

"It will mean that I will have to spend a lot more time with you, Malcolm. You will also get to see me in action again."

"Every cloud has a silver lining then," Malcolm giggled.

When his father came striding toward them the conversation dissolved. Although not making eye contact, Jen passed Daniel a coffee as he slid his chair right up next to her getting her very flustered. Then he slammed his hand down on her thigh, digging into it under the table which caused her to rear back.

"So, what's the game plan for today fellas?" Daniel asked enthusiastically across to them.

"I have to go with the Inspector to give him some background information on the body. It was that Lord Bellington and I know a bit about him," Malcolm mentioned to his father.

"I don't need to hire in a lawyer to watch over my son do I, Inspector?"

"No, it is purely an informal interview Sir."

"So that then leaves you and me, my little Brit, to find something to get up to," Daniel muttered.

"I have to help Inspector Atkinson with his case too," Jen said firmly.

Swiftly she turned with pleading eyes, toward the Inspector before she continued,

"It appears there are inconsistencies in my statement, typical me eh I can never get anything exactly right, how stupid can I be?"

The main door slowly opened and then Jane bounded in carrying a tennis racket.

"Oh, look your playmate of the month has arrived, to keep you busy," Jen sarcastically remarked.

"Morning Jane, we are just having breakfast do you want to join us?" Daniel called over to her.

"Yes, that would be great, move along everybody" Jan replied and bounced across the richly carpeted room.

"I am so glad you have come. You can have my place, I was leaving to go and change," Jen said, "I will be with you guys shortly."

With that Jen moved off and once more plunged herself into the wardrobe where she found a pair of extremely long jeans and an oversized shirt. Putting this outfit together was proving a challenge, but by rolling up the trouser legs and shirt sleeves, as well as borrowing a belt everything appeared to fit. Next, she found an old black pair of boots and put them on. Feeling rather proud of herself she strode back into the lounge, to meet up with Inspector Atkinson and Malcolm at the front door.

Not having to actually be with the Inspector, Jen quickly excused herself and took a walk around the boat. Trundling along a corridor she suddenly felt goosebumps prickling up along her arms and turning around she swore she saw a shadowy figure jump behind a large plant pot with a Rubber tree in it. Cautiously she backed away and then gathered her speed, racing around the next corner she flew slap into Daniel and Jane.

"Hey my little Brit what's the hurry?" asked Daniel. Jen explained she had just been a bit startled by something.

"What was it?" Daniel inquired.

His lips twitched in amusement at her wide-eyed expression.

"Nothing probably, I am just being silly," Jen responded nervously. "I am not comfortable in new environments; it always takes me a while to get my bearings."

"Yeah, I have realized that about you already, you have to introduce Mustangs to new environments slowly otherwise it makes them really skittish. Come with us and play some tennis. It will help take your mind off the case," Daniel said soothingly.

"I am a Master at tennis," Jen replied matter-of-factly. "But no thanks, I am not dressed for it. I will go back to the suite and have a little lie-down or maybe some breakfast will revive me."

Suddenly, Daniel glanced up and down her body before declaring,

"Are those my pants you have on?"

Quickly he turned her around, quite roughly and checked the label.

"You women, I don't mind you borrowing my car, wearing my shirts or even using my razor but not the pants or the shoes, a guy spends a lot of time of time *breaking* those items *in*."

Twirling around to face him, Jen's eyes flashed angrily and he laughed as she snorted at him, her nostrils flaring. He had started using that *breaking in phrase again* which really fired her up.

"Hey, they were in the wardrobe, the one you said I could use, how was I to know the difference?" Jen snapped as Jane stood back softly laughing, mockingly at her appearance.

"You are to go straight back to the suite and change," he declared assertively. "Move it."

Then Daniel turned to Jane to offer his apologies.

"I am going to have to take a rain check on this game sorry, I have another one to play."

Jane felt a sudden stab of jealousy as she watched them go, Daniel was clearly smitten.

Hurriedly he caught up with Jen, who was striding erratically ahead of him.

"Don't you turn around and look at me my little Brit keep moving."

Jen felt very alarmed that he was actually herding her along, at every corner he was there before her ushering and guiding her direction. Finally, when she flounced back into the suite Daniel was already there to open the door. Deliberately she stomped down in his boots hard as she marched up the stairs into his bedroom, to show her annoyance.

When he arrived behind her, in the doorway, she used the back of the boot to kick the bedroom door shut upon him.

The Inspector arrived and called up to Daniel,

"Hi Sir, we have had some news on the case. Malcolm has been very helpful, you should be very proud of him, he showed real courage today and made a valiant effort to answer a barrage of questions."

Blushing Malcolm sat down, before Ron continued, "The coroner has reported that Lord Bellington's death was caused by strangulation. Our investigation now takes a more sinister turn. Jen will have to be guarded twenty-four hours as she is the only one to have had contact with the killer. I am thinking of having her removed from the boat."

Alarmed at the prospect, Daniel spun around to look over at him.

"Surely that won't be necessary Inspector. We are taking care of her here just fine and you have my word she won't leave the suite again if you think that is necessary. I am sure I can keep her busy enough here," Daniel gloated, strolling over into the kitchen area and sitting at the table.

"If you're positive that won't be of any inconvenience to you Sir? You could be exposing yourself also to great danger," Ron queried.

Resolutely, Daniel confirmed to the Inspector that the current *arrangements* were *fine* and he felt *well prepared* to deal with any threat that might unfold.

Then Malcolm also chipped in, "It will mean you have to visit here a lot Inspector."

That settled it for Ron and he too became quite happy with the *arrangements* and accepted Malcolm's kind offer to stay for lunch. As they started to make the meal Ron looked around to Daniel to ask where Jen was now.

"The last time I saw her she was stomping around in our bedroom. I told her off for wearing my long pants as well as my shoes. Man, some women take advantage, don't they?"

Noting Daniel's annoyance, Ron nodded his head in agreement.

"Yeah for sure Sir. Your trousers and your shoes, wow some things a gentleman has to have kept private, to himself, for his exclusive use only. It makes me glad I haven't got a woman around who does that."

Rolling his eyes, Malcolm continued chopping up the vegetables as Jen entered wearing the cream linen dress again.

"I can't believe what a fuss you made," she declared loudly to Daniel.

"No, he has a point, Jen, some things are just sacred," replied the Inspector sitting down and stretching out his legs to observe his recently newly bought leather pointed shoes.

"Well, have me arrested then!" she snapped back. "I certainly wouldn't mind you borrowing any of my stuff."

"I don't think I would fit into any of yours." Daniel chuckled.

Malcolm hooted with laughter before replying to his father,

"You should give it a go dad; you may find it a complete revelation. You should speak to my friends Jen; I am sure they won't mind lending you some stuff."

Given that Jen had already checked out their stuff, she shuffled nervously on her feet.

"You mean your fruit salad, Malcolm. Hardly, they barely wear anything at all. I may as well simply sit here naked."

"Now that would be a revelation worth experiencing," Daniel joked.

Passing around the salad, he had so carefully prepared, Malcolm joined the others to eat. When Jen finished preparing the food on her plate, Daniel suddenly took it from her and she snorted before making herself up another one.

Carefully Daniel poured them all some wine, though Inspector Atkinson declined, he was still officially on duty. The girls arrived still damp from the pool and began joining in, taking their food to the couch and putting on the TV.

"I thought you were going to take a nap, Jen?" Daniel murmured.

"Every time I settle down for a sleep in this boat, bodies start either tumbling on to me or I fall on to them," she moaned. "I will just sit here and force myself to keep awake until the Inspector gives me permission to leave."

"I have some favourable news on that score, Jen," Ron mentioned. "Lord Bellington was strangled and so we have a murderer aboard the boat. Detectives are still questioning everyone but I am happy to say you will be staying here, under guard, until the killer is apprehended. You are not allowed to leave this suite."

  After finishing her meal Jen got up and started pacing around the room. Malcolm commented on this, wondering if she would ever just settle down and relax, she was wearing out the carpet.

"She just needs to be taken out and given a long hard ride," his father mumbled, strumming his fingers on the table.

"Dad, are you going through the change or something? I know you hit fifty later this year but really, I thought it was only women who went through some sort of alteration with all those hot flushes."

"I hit thirty-five this year myself, getting on a bit as well," Ron commented getting up and stretching his limbs.

"No, that is such a lovely age Inspector," Malcolm cooed over admiring his physique. "Well, why don't we play a game of cards that will kill a bit of time?"

Aimlessly, Daniel continued watching Jen pacing up and down the lounge whilst slowly munched down on some crisps from a bowl, his head tilted resting on his hand. Happily, Malcolm invited the other girls to join him and they readily agreed, turning he called Jen over.

"Sorry, of course, why not, I am a Master at card games! Who is going to deal?" she asked excitedly.

Apricot took the deck and spread it around in a circle, then Cherry and Strawberry begin to stack the cards up on top of each other.

Strawberry giggled.

"We love trying to build a tower with them, but it is so delicate we rarely succeed."

"Not many rules to this game then," Jen snorted.

However, Malcolm joined the game, laughing with them as they tried to build a tower.

Annoyed, Jen blew her hair out of her face before getting up and starting to pace about again. After sometime Daniel suddenly blocked her path and ordered her to go to bed, promising to stand guard. Finally, he raised a finger and pointed it at her declaring,

"Now don't you snort at me my little Mustang or I will carry you up there again."

Trying to remain calm, Jen simply shrugged her shoulders, sighed and wandered up to the room. Plonking herself in the middle of the bed, she curled up into a ball and soon fell asleep.

Chapter 6: Keep an Open Mind

Upon waking she found Daniel unsurprisingly asleep next to her. Trying to be very slow and quiet in her movements, she delicately shifted herself across the bed in order to get off it, but Daniel felt the movement beneath him and rolled over.

"I can see you are admitting defeat then," Daniel said raising his head. "I win round three without having to even make any effort."

"This is all such a game and a laugh to you isn't it Daniel?"

But he replied light-heartedly, "Sure it's the best game ever......the game of life. Life should be one great adventure and challenge don't you think my little Brit?"

Playfully he snatched her up and pushed her underneath him.

"And you love to conqueror all, is that right Daniel?" Jen retorted, trying to wriggle out from beneath him as he bent forward and whispered in her ear, "I like to take control of things my little Mustang, can't wait to break you in making you subservient in the bedroom."

Alarmed Jen's responded in an assertive manner, "As if that is going to happen. Okay well, this is going to be over in a few minutes again then."

"I am ready and rearing to go," Daniel declared challengingly. "I don't see why you are all riled up. We both got one round in each and that sort of keeps us even, neck and neck." Easily pushing him off her she clambered off the bed.

Spinning round Jen snorted at him though and stamped her foot. This sent him into a complete fit of laughter, which perplexed her. Striding off into the walk-in wardrobe she changed back into the linen dress.

Returning to the room, she found him pretending to sleep, so she left. Finding the place had been deserted, she walked to the fridge to pour herself a glass of juice and then exited the suite. Heading toward the incident room, Jen found Malcolm and Inspector Atkinson sitting together.

"Hey, you are meant to be in the suite Jen. I told Mr. Stapleton not to leave you alone," Ron remarked as he finished writing up some notes.

"Believe me, Inspector, I am far safer out here with a murderer on the loose, then back in there with him," Jen choked out, to the bemused pair.

"Got his lasso out did he?" laughed Malcolm, pretending that he had one by swirling his hand in the air.

"Oh shit, I didn't know he had one of those. No, I still have that pleasure to come then. Any joys here?"

"It has been all go here Jen, hasn't it Inspector. It transpires that Lord Bellington may have been killed by a spurned lover! This is more exciting than the TV show *The Bold and the Beautiful*! Inspector Atkinson is currently busy cross-checking the names of all the men on board, who may have had any connection with him and I am his assistant."

Begrudgingly, Ron commented that they hadn't had any luck so far so Jen must continue to watch her back. Then Jen complained that she could not be expected to sit in that suite all day, admitting to not being able to sit still for more than thirty minutes at best.

"You wouldn't be a great date to take to the movies then." Malcolm giggled.

"The complete worst date imaginable Malcolm. I am heading off to the top deck to clear my head."

It was a bit of an overcast day and not many people were up on deck as Jen took her stroll. Whilst meandering about she began to feel that someone was watching her again. This unnerved her slightly, so she went back to the door where she had come from but found it locked. Looking up she saw a murky figure approach her, startled she ran off. Jen galloped around the deck at high speed, before eventually hiding inside a small equipment shelter, breathing heavily she peeked out.

A man jogged passed in a dark tracksuit with a cap on his head. Abruptly, she squatted down for fear he might return. Peeping out again she noticed a small child skip by and then a lady, with frizzy, long ginger hair, shortly followed behind the child. Slipping out she eventually found an exit door, opening it she took the steps two at a time. Realizing she was now lost inside the ship, added to her sense of fear though, until she came across a Steward who was more than happy to direct her back to the suite. Arriving, looking flustered, Daniel approached her first.

 "You really pushed the boundaries today didn't you, my little Brit. You know you weren't supposed to leave the suite and yet you bolted."

"I met up with Inspector Atkinson and Malcolm actually, I was perfectly safe," she snapped back at him.

"The Inspector and Malcolm are here, look. Everyone has been waiting for you and worrying about you. You deserve a good spanking," Daniel shouted.

 Throwing back her head she glared at him challengingly before she retorted,

 "As if! I did go out for some fresh air; it's meant to be a healthy thing to do and then I did run into a slight problem, to tell the truth. I had an uncomfortable feeling I was being followed and then when I returned from the deck, I found the door locked. Not that I was frightened of course but somebody seemed to run at me and that did make me take off. Just silly nonsense of course!"

"That is the last straw, I am going to have to use my lasso," Daniel commented walking around her.

"Malcolm warned me about that. I wondered when it was going to make an appearance. What an earth will you do with it?" asked Jen backing away from him anxiously.

"Don't even tempt me to answer that my little Mustang, suffice to say you aren't to leave my side again," he snarled at her.

"Inspector Atkinson only said I wasn't to leave the suite," she called over her shoulder to him hurrying over to join Ron and Malcolm.

When she served herself up some pasta, Daniel walked up behind her and snatched it, so she served herself another bowl.

Then Daniel remarked to the others, "I am still training her. She is a work in progress."

Taking up his fork to eat, Jen settled herself down at the table with them.

"My little Brit got jumped on today Inspector, she will have to write you up a statement about it."

"I never said that Daniel," Jen replied flushed and turned to the Inspector. "I thought I was being chased up on deck earlier, but it may have simply been an innocent jogger. I can't even give you a specific description of him so what is the point?"

"The point is you stay here in the suite, where no one can get to you," Ron stated firmly.

"Apart from me," Daniel sniggered and heartily tucked into his meal.

"And there is no escaping you, dad," Malcolm quipped. "Okay Jen, borrow my laptop after supper and check up on your emails that should keep you busy for at least thirty minutes".

Playfully, he winked at her.

"Thanks for that Malcolm. I do always worry about what is going on at work, particularly when I am not there to supervise, there is usually something going on and I have to keep up with their antics."

"I have noticed already that you are quite skeptical by nature," Daniel informed her. "Horses are also skeptical creatures you know."

With that Malcolm reprimanded his father yet again, about his comment, before going off to fetch his laptop. Returning speedily to the dining table to set it up for Jen to use. Quite content, Jen sat at the table working away and Daniel brought his laptop to sit beside her.

"Just so you realize Daniel I do actually have work to do. Questioning all the work that has been covered in my absence and forwarded on to me. No distractions," she warned him.

"No sorry I didn't quite catch that. You have to actually make eye contact with me, my little Mustang, when you speak to me it is part of your training. It means that you have learned to trust me and no snorting or grinding your teeth, I heard that" Daniel remarked.

The Inspector made his excuses and left them. Malcolm followed him out to say goodbye in private.

"Well that is disappointing, everything at work seems to be ticking along, nothing for me to review at all. Clare simply writes *it's all quiet and peaceful here without you, don't stress about us. Relax and enjoy the holiday, the boss even says you can extend it*. What is she implying with that statement? I think I should reply giving her a piece of my mind," she said but Daniel pushed down the lid of the laptop.

"Never best to reply to emails when you are in a jumpy state. Here let me give you a massage you had a shock today and just need to calm down," he said in soft low tones.

"That was quite impertinent of you Daniel. I like to make my own mind up of what my next course of action should be," Jen declared.

Getting out of his chair Daniel started rubbing her shoulders, which did help relax her for a few minutes.

"Yes, I know you do, now come over here to the couch or do I have to put a halter on you?" he asked harshly.

"You really have this thing about me being like a Mustang, don't you?" she replied wistfully.

Daniel took her hand and gently pulled on it, he spoke to her reassuringly,

"I know you're stressed, it's okay come quietly, a massage will relax you. It was a hectic day for you so you do just need to now quieten down."

Still enjoying the shoulder rub, Jen responded to this by getting up and muttering to herself that it had in fact been a very tiring day, allowing herself to lay on her stomach, on the couch so he could then begin his magic. The gentle rub soon succeeded in sending her off to sleep.

Resting her head gently in his lap, he turned the TV on and occasionally glanced down at her, stroking her hair when she stirred to settle her.

"I can see you are making some progress with her then," Malcolm said, quietly closing the door behind him and walking back into the room. "Where is this all going though dad? We will all be leaving in a few days and I am sure you are going to go back to those precious horses of yours. You must miss them dreadfully!"

"Surprisingly not quite as much as I usually do Malcolm. I am going to have to devise some cunning plan to take her back home with us, eh, son. I get the feeling she is a little lost foal anyway, in need of a good home."

"Wow, you have been well and truly bitten by that love bug dad," Malcolm sighed, observing them on the couch.

"Yeah. I wish the same for you to son. It's great to have a partner in your life, someone you can depend on and feel secure with."

Swiftly Daniel glanced up at Malcolm, who was still leaning over the back of the couch watching them.

"Life isn't so straight forward for me, dad. Sometimes I feel like a tortured soul, doomed to roam the earth as a single man forever," Malcolm complained, walking around and dumping himself on a rug, placed in front of the flat-screen TV.

"You are being very melodramatic as usual Malcolm probably because you are gay," stated his father.

Jumping up on to his knees Malcolm faced his dad, his cheeks burning red.

"Dad, did you just say that I was gay?" Malcolm responded, feeling very flustered.

"That Andy Bell, Erasure period you went through in your teens never really left you did it, son. Listen I wouldn't want to change you Malcolm you mean everything to me so let's cut to the chase. I love you and I want you to be happy. Relationships take a lot of work; my little Brit here still needs to wake up to the fact she is even in one but I will get there eventually with her."

Daniel gazed across to Malcolm who was shyly looking down.

"So, you are saying you are comfortable with me being gay dad?"

To which Daniel nodded his head and said, "I am glad you have found yourself, Malcolm. I hope now you can go about finding your feet, so you can settle down and start taking on some responsibility in your life. Start making your own way. It is what every father wants for his child. I am no different."

Coming forward, to hug his father, Malcolm declared how much he loved him and that he wished they had had this conversation years ago to which Daniel agreed. Malcolm bent over to hug his dad and then they settled down to watch a TV show before Daniel carried a very sleepy Jen up to his bedroom and snuggled up next to her.

Chapter 7: Time & Care Needed

The following morning Daniel began to feel Jen stir and he nuzzled up against her as she looked up at him all bleary-eyed.

"I loved feeling your breath on me last night my little Brit. I feel like I have finally found someone that I connect with," Daniel whispered and placed his face next to hers.

"Daniel, I think you are going through one of your fads," she replied sitting up. "Once all this excitement has died down, you will return to your natural habitat and settle down to your usual routine again. Back to your old roguish ways, I am sure."

"You still have a lot to discover about me and we still have a lot of time ahead of us for you to do that," he commented laying back on the silk pillowcases.

"I am not going to let you break me, Daniel," she stated casting her eyes downwards.

"I think you misunderstand my meaning of that phrase. For you it seems to mean a break of spirit, I would never want that to happen. You just need basic relationship training did you ever learn to share as a child?" he asked. Jen stated that she was, in fact, an only child and he commented that this explained a lot about her.

"Surely this is just a holiday fling for you Daniel."

 "Not wanting to freak you out but I have come to adore you." He swiftly replied. "but I know you need time to adjust. Life can be lonely; it's certainly not been boring with you. Partner up with me."

"That's the statement that gets to me, Daniel. Being someone's."

"Yeah I get that about you," Daniel remarked. "But as I say I am continuing with my basic training, so that eventually you may start allowing yourself to be more open to it. You are such a little Mustang. Now, what do I always like to have in the morning?"

"It's a black coffee, isn't it Daniel?"

He smiled broadly.

"That's right, good girl."

"I respond well to positive language Daniel. Yes, I do consider myself a good girl, at work some people can be so negative at times."

Smirking he turned and pulled onto the bed a large gift-wrapped parcel and placed it in front of her. "I have a gift for you by the way."

Suspiciously Jen stared at it for a while.

"You're meant to open it," he urged her.

However, Jen became quite put out, stuttering, "Wwwell I don't know what it can possibly be, or why I suddenly deserve a gift!"

"Jen really, people who have feelings for each other do this kind of thing," he murmured, taking up her hand and kissing the back of it. "You're such a skeptic, I have no ulterior motives other than to express my love for you."

"That is very kind of you and I do realize that Daniel. I have been given presents before, at Christmas and my birthdays. I don't want you to think that I am ungrateful, it has caught me off guard a bit that's all. My parents usually put some money into my account for me to buy my own. Well, I will have to be brave and open it, oh wow, ah, I so love this. A pair of jeans my size, some black cowboy boots, and an olive-green shirt. Olive green is so my favourite colour. How did you know that?" she asked him questioningly.

Chuckling Daniel said, "That color reminded me of the grasslands around my ranch."

"This is actually very thrilling; I like this present thanks, Daniel. Oh, and the shirt has some writing on the back. *My little Mustang,* that is a bit unusual but no, on the whole, you did very well there, well-done. Normally I get given gift vouchers, by close friends, apparently, I am a difficult person to buy for. I can get a bit critical but you certainly have proven you are getting to know me. So, can I give you a hug then?"

Swiftly he moved forward to accept her embrace, before she went off to the bathroom, with her gift to change into.

Meeting up with Malcolm in the kitchen, Jane showed off her new outfit and then made herself a coffee, while he continued cooking. When Daniel arrived, Jen placed his coffee mug beside him as he sat down and patted the seat next to him indicating for her to sit. However, she remained standing shifting about on her feet.

"Come eat, Malcolm has made some burgers," he ordered.

"I am vegetarian, so obviously I won't be eating any of those," Jen responded sternly.

"No, you can eat those, they aren't made of meat, we gave up eating meat long ago," Malcolm said cheerfully. "All those nasty things that are added to your food these days. We want to do our bit to save the planet. You aren't the only vegetarian in the world you know."

"But I thought you Americans loved your meat!" Jen commented looking in disbelief at the pair of them.

"You are stereotyping us, that's a bad girl," Daniel said assertively and he turned to point his finger at her.

"Pointing fingers is considered very rude in Britain," Jen mentioned.

"Yeah well, I left my lunge rope back in the States. Now come and sit down next to me. Couples do sit together here; that is not illegal in Britain is it to sit with your partner?"

Sitting next to Daniel she carefully prepared a burger for herself adding salad, fried onions, and some sauce to the side of her plate.   Once again Daniel took the plate from her so she had to prepare another one.

"I love the way you serve me my food Jen, I will give you a massage later to say thank you."

Resigned, Jen understood from this that Daniel was on one of his training sessions with her again. Although Jen found Daniel's lessons a bit patronizing as she felt she did know how to share, she found herself complying with them. Lately, Jen had become more open to wondering about what life would be like living with Daniel. He was a very impulsive creature who defiantly challenged her in ways she hadn't come across before. His mischievous behaviour both amused and bemused her, which was in itself intriguing. Life with him would be a stampede of endless witticisms, which appealed to her. It had struck her that after this whirlwind romance had ended and she returned to her treadmill existence she would feel quite desolate.

Admitting to herself that she was bored *shitless* at work, the predictable monotonous tasks she mechanically went through every day. Returning back to an environment where others imposed their sanctimonious monologues upon her, succeeding in making her feel completely obsolete. Did Daniel offer her a chance to move on to greener pastures?

"You two just kill me, I will choke on this burger if you don't stop," Malcolm interjected. "I promised to bring Inspector Atkinson up a coffee so I will see you later. Try and play nicely while I am gone."

Over the course of the next few days, Jen and Daniel became quite inseparable. The Inspector relented allowing Jan to leave the suite when accompanied by Daniel. They went to the casino, where she noted with relief, he appeared quite the shrewd gambler. At the poolside movie theatre, Daniel was his usual mischievous self. His abrasive character made her nerves jangle but in an exhilarated way and Jen felt that the cruise had lived up to its promise to *revive* her. Being ravished by Daniel was also definitely quite refreshing, with all his attention to detail!

Chapter 8: Think About The Future

As the days passed, with no news from the Inspector as to how the case was progressing, Malcolm and Jen devised a plan to flush the murderer out. Given that there was a party being held by the Captain that night, to cheer everyone up, they felt it was the perfect opportunity to solve this case.

Later that day everyone gathered in the hallway to take part in this event. Unfortunately, Jen and Malcolm noted that the Spanish matador outfits that they had chosen to wear, with the words *SAVE THE BULLS* emblazoned on them, were at slight odds with this pirate-themed party. The number of stuffed parrots on shoulders was a clear clue. Undeterred they took to the dance floor and mingled with other guests. Daniel entered looking very slick in a tuxedo, the Pirate theme appeared to have been overlooked by him also.

Undeterred their plan, to draw out the killer, was put into action. Dancing around to the Erasure song *Love to hate You*, Malcolm was in his element. Then Daniel danced with Jen to *Meatloaf's* hit song *Midnight at the lost and found* which put everyone in the party spirit. Not letting their guard down, cautiously Jan and Malcolm kept an eye out on who might try and entangle himself with her. A gingered haired waitress appeared to try and bump into Jen on several occasions, but Daniel carefully stepped into overt any mishaps. Then a man with a long dangling beard appeared before her.

Given that he didn't have the traditional parrot on his shoulder, more of a manky eagle with two heads, Jen's suspicions were heightened.

Asking her to dance, in a thick accent, that Jen couldn't place was slightly disconcerting as well but she politely agreed. Swiftly, Malcolm pulled

Daniel away, declaring that he was spoiling everything.

After the dance, the bearded man led Jen away from the crowd to a quiet secluded table.

Discretely, Daniel and Malcolm placed themselves a few tables away.

"Thank you for that dance," Jen stated. "I am not usually into the *Macarena* song but that was quite fun." Then getting straight down to business she went on, "Did you hear about that murder on the boat the other day."

"Yes," the man appeared to hiss back at her. "Word has it that it was your room the body was found in. There has been a lot of talk about it. Where I come from murders happen every day though."

Fidgeting nervously on her seat, Jen did not know what to make of that statement. "Well, it's very unusual for Southampton I am sure. Not that I come from around here myself."

"I have been watching you," the man continued producing a bottle of whiskey from his coat and two shot glasses. Offering her a glass she shook her head, but he quickly downed two shots of it before continuing, "You maybe want to come up onto the deck with me. For how you say, a stroll. I saw you up there the other day. You were running about, upset maybe?"

It was definitely him, Jen surmised but what should she do now? The bearded man began drinking again, his pleasant demeanor appeared to diminish and he began looking a bit bleary-eyed. Trying to play it cool she replied, "The Inspector said I was not to go off with strangers, thank you very much."

However, the bearded man was not to be put off so lightly and he proceeded to take up her hand attempting to kiss it. Given his inebriated state, this proved quite a challenge. But this action caused Daniel to shoot up in his seat with Malcolm hot on his heels.

Quick as a flash Daniel pulled Jen up by her arm and whisked her away.

They bumped into the Inspector at the door.

"Thank God it's you, inspector, we have found our culprit. The bearded man at the table over there, he must have been the one pursuing me on the deck the other day. He practically admitted it."

"Have you been playing detective again. That is a very dangerous game." The inspected stated solemnly.

"Don't blame her. It was my fault; we devised this plan to flush the murderer out. Unfortunately, it seems to have worked." Malcolm whined.

"Now now, I am sure you were both trying to be very brave and courageous, but putting yourself in harm's way will only hinder this investigation. Besides it can't be him, he is a monk from Russia and is sworn to silence. Interviewing him was extremely challenging. He ended up drawing pictures"

They surveyed the bearded man.

"Well he has broken his vow of silence," Jen mentioned. "So, you might find it a bit easier now."

"I have had enough of Russian interference, let me have a few words with him." Daniel snarled rolling up his sleeves, but the Inspector ushered them away.

They wandered over to the bar for a drink. Malcolm ordered a decaf coffee and apologized once again for hindering the investigation. Still quite emotional, he mentioned he was feeling tired. Collecting his drink, he left the group to return to the suite.

Wandering down the corridor Malcolm noticed the ginger-haired lady again, but this time she was not dressed in her bunny outfit waitress costume and appeared to be engaged in a heated argument with a Steward. They then actually started fighting. Malcolm froze on the spot, the woman with frizzy hair suddenly produced a knife and plunged it into the man.

Dropping the coffee cup, in horror, Malcolm quickly turned on his heels. Rushing back toward the bar with the screams of the injured man still ringing in his ears, he burst into the room.

"Dad, dad I witnessed a murder, quick get the Inspector. A woman stabbed a man down the corridor and I saw it. Quick phone for help," he wailed.

Shooting up from his seat Daniel reacted quickly.

"Malcolm I will go and check out the scene and try to find the Inspector. You go back to the suite with my little Brit and watch over the fruit salad. Bolt the door until I return."

Much to Malcolm's despair, the ladies were not in his apartment, so he rushed off to find them, leaving Jen alone. Forgetting to lock the door Jen began to pace about nervously. Hearing a screech, she turned to see the frizzy ginger-haired woman racing toward her, from the balcony door, in a wild manner, wielding a knife.

Gathering herself Jen shouted across to her,

"I should warn you; I am a Master at boxing."

Putting up her fists as the woman approached her. She lashed out a punch at her but missed spectacularly, then her fist did hit the enraged woman, on the side of the chin and the lady buckled to the ground.

"Oh, that really hurt, my hand is throbbing now. Oh shit," Jen shrieked. Momentarily she began nursing it but then recovering herself quickly when she noticed the woman regain her composure. Screeching and snarling again the culprit rushed at her again.

Frantically Jen leaped about the room, knocking into furniture to avoid her lunges. Meanwhile, Malcolm had hurried frantically into the incident room.

"There's been another murder."

Racing with Inspector Atkinson and other policemen back to where the incident took place, his dad was kneeling over the body of the Steward.

Daniel was holding a towel firmly over the bloody wound.

"He is not dead but will need immediate medical attention."

The police cordoned off the scene to secure it.

"We will take it from here Sir," Ron told Daniel. "Take Malcolm back to your suite, look after him, he is very shaken up."

"No, I am fine Inspector really," Malcolm stated breathlessly.

"Well you are a braver man than me then," Ron replied and Malcolm blushed.

Back at the suite, the girls returned and wandered into a bedroom. When Cherry opened the door of their bedroom again, she found Jen hurtling toward it, shouting for them to close the door and lock it, so she did. Jen slammed herself on to the now closed-door shouting,

"You were meant to let me in you idiots."

A knife suddenly pierced into the door panel by her cheek and she bolted toward the balcony. The deranged woman screamed hysterically pulling it out of the door frame and pursued her.

Climbing up on to some plastic slats, Jen scampered up along the lining of the boat but she was slipping badly and found it difficult to hold on. The madwoman was attempting to reach her, with the knife being held between her teeth but she too was skidding. Jen had started yelling for help when Malcolm and Daniel arrived in the suite. Upon hearing her frantic cries, they dashed out to the balcony and looked up.

"Go and get the Inspector. I will meet you up on deck Malcolm."

Grabbing his lasso Daniel ran out of the suite, up a flight of stairs and on to the deck, where he could see both women below him. He called out for Jen to look up, which she did.

"Daniel thank God, this lunatic is trying to kill me help," she called out. Glancing down below her she panicked realizing that she would never survive such a drop.

"Don't look down Jen, I am going to throw the rope for you catch it and I will pull you up."

Finally, Malcolm and the Inspector arrived beside Daniel. The culprit swiftly grabbed at Jen's foot and pulled on it, which dislodged her completely. Suddenly Jen's whole body began to veer backward, she shrieked out as her hands no longer had anything to hold on to and were flailing about in the air above her head.

Hollering out for everyone to stand back, Daniel hurled the lasso upwards. Knowing he only had one go at this, he twirled it around.

Shock penetrated through her body and then she heard a whooshing sound, Daniel's lasso looped in the air, bracing itself over her back. When it tightened around her body, she found herself dangling, swaying wilding in mid-air then she slammed back onto the slates as Daniel winched her in.

"That was an extremely good shot, Sir," bellowed the Inspector.

Feeling elated Malcolm cried out, "My dad is a Master with the lasso Inspector. Oh, I have the sound of *The Big Country theme tune* still ringing in my ears, after that heart-stopping moment, it's one of Dad's favorites. Oh, up she comes."

Helplessly, Jen reached out and Daniel pulled her in, checking she was okay before hugging her, she certainly relished such attentive behaviour. In a rush of emotions, she realized she had reached a pivotal point in her life, a chance to take the reins and kissed him tentatively.

Daniel's heart skipped a beat, knowing he had finally managed to rope in her heart.

"What about her? Quick Daniel throw down your lasso," Jen cried out.

Obediently, Daniel threw it down again, pulling up the now breathless woman, who was promptly placed in handcuffs and escorted away by the Police.

"You do realize that was Lady Bellington," Ron declared. "Good grief, well I will catch up with you later, more interrogations to be getting on with."

After Malcolm waved him off, he then watched his dad taking Jen in his arms again, he gazed warmly at them.

The following morning Jen, Daniel, and Malcolm were gathered around the table eating breakfast. Inspector Atkinson marched in, took off his coat and discarded it on the arm of the sofa.

"Good morning everyone, I trust you slept well after the hectic events of last night?" he asked.

Running forward Malcolm gave him a hug and stated that they were all fine. Happily, Malcolm invited the Inspector to join them and he accepted.

"Make me a coffee please Malcolm, you should know how I take it by now," Ron said quite assertively. "You will all be relieved to know that you no longer have to remain in this suite and are free to leave the ship. You will need to be contactable, however, so you can't travel out of the country quite yet.

I am afraid Malcolm you will have to appear in court, at the hearing of Lady Bellington, who has confessed all. She apparently murdered her husband in a jealous rage and when she departed the original murder scene, she didn't realize she hadn't actually been seen by you, Jen. Unfortunately for her, she was however seen by one of the stewards who promptly started blackmailing her. To rid herself of this parasite, she attempted to kill him off too, but he is still alive and should make a complete recovery. However, he will of course then go directly to jail for his part in all of this. Once Malcolm saw her trying to kill the Steward, she then clambered into his suite to kill him and ended up attacking you."

"Well, she was after me anyway. Killing two birds with one stone, I suppose. Attempting to murder me on the deck and then again at the party."

"Quite." The inspector put in.

"I am just relieved it is all over," Malcolm chimed in handing Ron his coffee. "The last thing we want is dead bodies all over the place. There are usually several in all the TV crime shows I watch. My dad has taken up an apartment around here, so I am sure we will be spending a lot more time together Inspector, I mean Ron."

"And I look forward to it," Ron replied cheerfully.

"I too have some news. My little Brit has consented to come back to the states with me." Daniel beamed. "I am looking forward to showing off our ranch to her. I am hoping you are a Master at horse riding," he said turning to Jen.

"I do like to think of myself as an accomplished rider, yes Daniel but no one ever really gets to Master the horse. They are very challenging beasts you see. Never underestimate a horse but I thought you would have known that already. I understand however that in America you ride horses in rather an unusual fashion so I am going to enjoy teaching you the correct technique. More coffee anyone?"

Raising an eyebrow, Daniel slowly began wagging his finger at her as Ron and Malcolm, laughingly watched on.

Epilogue

Some months on, Ron and Malcolm showed off their own wedding rings to guests, following their rather formally attired, civil ceremony in London.

In turn, a few weeks later, they then watched Miss Jen Appleton become Mrs. Jen Stapleton at a service held at Daniel's ranch in America. A less formal affair, with all his *valued* horses in attendance. Life indeed seemed idyllic, until the fateful day that Malcolm and Jen unwittingly discovered a dismembered body in the library and then it all descended into shenanigans once again!

"Dad, dad there's been another murder!"

THE END

Printed in Great Britain
by Amazon